Against the Odds

JOE LAYDEN

Against the Odds

JOE LAYDEN

SCHOLASTIC INC.

NEW YORK   TORONTO   LONDON   AUCKLAND   SYDNEY

Not AR

B
J 796.323 64
LAY

Basketball
- profession
- biography
- sports - basketball

10/99 6:7

PHOTO CREDITS

Cover (Miller), 2, 37, 47, 71: NBA/Nathaniel S. Butler. **Cover (background)**,
61, 77: NBA/Andrew D. Bernstein. 1, 3: NBA/Barry Gossage.
4, 57: NBA/Juan O'Campo. 5, 27, 81: NBA/Lou Capozzola.
7: NBA/Fernando Medina. 13: NBA Photo Library.
17: NBA/Allen Einstein. 21: NBA/Sam Forencich. 31, 43: NBA/Steve Woltman.
52: NBA/Noren Trotman. 67: NBA/Glenn James.

PHOTO CREDITS: INSERT SECTION

I **(Anderson)**: NBA/Fernando Medina. II **(Gatling)**, VI **(Mullin)**: NBA/Andy Hayt.
III **(Kerr)**: NBA/Tim Defrisco. IV **(Miller)**: NBA/Frank McGrath.
V **(Mourning)**: NBA/Richard Lewis. VII **(Rogers)**: NBA/Louis Capozzola.
VIII **(Williams)**: NBA/Tim O'Dell.

ISBN 0-590-12082-4

© 1997 by NBA Properties, Inc.
All rights reserved. Published by Scholastic Inc.

12 11 10 9 8 7 6 5 4 3   8 9/9 0 1 2 3/0

Printed in the U.S.A.
First Scholastic printing, April 1998
Book design: Michael Malone

For my buddy Giacomo
—J.L.

TABLE OF CONTENTS

Against the Odds

Odds

JOE LAYDEN

INTRODUCTION

It takes more than just talent to make it to the NBA. It takes tremendous sacrifice and dedication—and perhaps a little luck. Millions of kids dream of playing professional basketball, but only a handful will see their dreams come true.

It's understood that everyone who wears an NBA uniform has spent countless hours in the gym. They've refined their skills through years of practice. They have a competitive edge sharpened by endless games and scrimmages. For some players, though, the journey has been particularly long and difficult. In addition to sweat, they have shed blood and tears. They've endured more heartache and hardship than many of us can imagine.

In this book, you'll read about some of these unique men. They are all successful NBA players. At first glance they seem to have everything: fame, wealth, happiness. They get to play basketball every day. And they get paid well for doing it. But there is much more beneath the surface. Look closely and you'll see that their lives have not been easy. These are some of the strongest men in professional sports, for they are survivors. They have overcome harsh and sometimes dangerous circumstances to achieve their goals. Their stories will surprise and inspire you.

Everyone knows Reggie Miller, right?  He's the confident, sharp-shooting All-Star for the Indiana Pacers. He seems to fear nothing. But did you know that Reggie had to wear braces on his legs when he was a little boy? Did you know that doctors questioned whether he'd ever be able to walk without a limp, let alone play basketball?

Reggie Miller

Did you know that Alonzo Mourning, the

Chris Gatling

muscular center for the Miami Heat, spent most of his childhood in foster homes?

Did you know that alcoholism nearly cost Chris Mullin his basketball career?

Chris Mullin

Did you know that Jayson Williams, one of the NBA's top rebounders, thought about quitting basketball when he was in college? He had lost both of his sisters to AIDS and was trying to help care for their two small children. The burden of responsibility almost prompted Jayson to give up.

But he didn't. In fact, not one of the eight players profiled on these pages has ever quit. They have all triumphed over adversity. Against overwhelming odds, they have made it to the top of the basketball world: the NBA! Though some of the stories in this book are sad, they are ultimately uplifting because they demonstrate the power of the human spirit. They prove that it's possible to rise above the bleakest situation.

There is always hope.

Jayson Williams

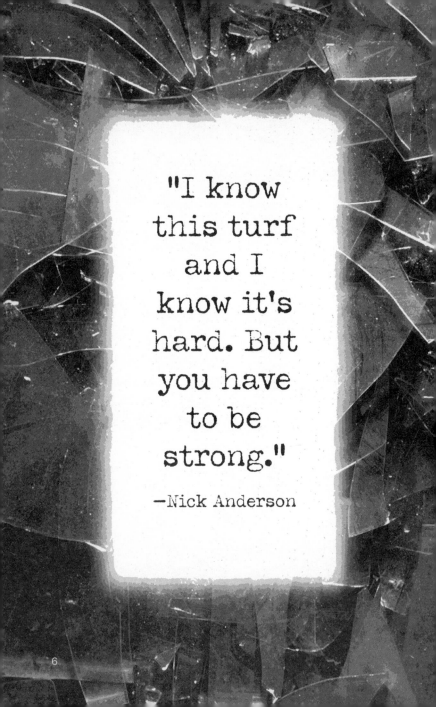

"I know this turf and I know it's hard. But you have to be strong."

—Nick Anderson

NICK
ANDERSON

A FRIEND
FOREVER

Before each home game, Orlando Magic guard Nick Anderson takes a long, slow ride from his neat suburban home to the Orlando Arena. Along the way, he passes through one of the roughest parts of the city—a poor, violent neighborhood much like the one in which he grew up. As he stares at the wooden shanties, the drug dealers, and the gang members, he realizes that he hasn't traveled so far after all. The streets are never far away.

"I take that ride because I don't ever want to forget how lucky I am," Nick says. "It keeps me focused on reality."

Today Nick is one of the top shooting guards in the NBA. He makes a lot of money playing a game he loves. For that he's extremely grateful. He knows things could have turned out differently—as they did for his best friend, Benjamin Wilson.

In the fall of 1984 Wilson was a senior at Neal F. Simeon Vocational High School in Chicago. A 6-8 forward with extraordinary athletic ability, he was generally considered the best high school basketball player in the nation. A year younger and a few inches shorter, Nick was also a promising young player from Chicago. He and Ben had gotten to know each other through playground games and summer camps. Along the way they had become close friends. So close, in fact, that Nick decided to transfer from Prosser Vocational to Simeon after his sophomore year, despite the fact that he would have to take a 90-minute bus ride to get to school each morning. That's how badly he wanted to play alongside his buddy.

"Benjy was Magic Johnson, but with a jump shot," Nick once told *The New York Times*. "He had all those moves. And he was so positive about everything. He used to record inspirational tapes for himself, and go to sleep with earphones, listening to himself saying, 'Ben, you're going to be the best.'"

With Benjy in the frontcourt and Nick in the backcourt, Simeon was rated the top high school team in the nation prior to the 1984–85 season. But tragedy prevented the two boys from ever playing a game together. On November 20, 1984, during a lunchtime break from school, Nick and Benjy were walking along South Vincennes Avenue. While Nick stopped inside a store to buy some candy, Benjy became involved in an argument with a pair of boys from another school. The confrontation quickly turned violent. One of the teens pulled out a pistol and shot Benjy in the chest and stomach.

From inside the store Nick could hear people screaming. As he ran out into the street, someone yelled, "Benjy's been shot!" Nick was shocked. He couldn't believe it. But it was true. He spotted his friend a short distance away, leaning against a fence, his coat covered with blood. Nick was frightened and angry. He felt helpless. All he could do was talk to Benjy while they waited for an ambulance to arrive.

Within minutes Benjy was on his way to a near-by hospital, where doctors worked feverishly to save his life. But there wasn't much they could do. The bullets had ripped into Benjy's heart and liver; there was simply too much damage.

On November 21, just a few hours after his death, a memorial service for Benjamin Wilson was held in the Simeon gymnasium. The next night Simeon played its first basketball game of the new season. Many of the players, including Nick Anderson, wept openly during pregame introductions. Later that week more than 8,000 people attended Benjy's wake and funeral. He was buried in his Simeon basketball uniform and warm-ups, with No. 25 across his chest.

The Comeback Kid

Nick was devastated by the death of his friend. He was scared and confused. For many months he often woke in the middle of the night, crying, shaking and sweating. He feared that he was losing his mind. Nick's parents were so concerned that they checked him into a local hospital, where he received psychological counseling. After two weeks he was released. It turned out that Nick was just a normal 16-year-old boy grieving over the terrible loss of a close friend. Now, though, it was time to get on with his life.

Nick was devastated by Benjy's death, often waking in the middle of the night, crying uncontrollably.

Nick led Simeon to the quarterfinals of the Illinois state tournament in his junior year; the next season Simeon went 25–1 and was the top-ranked team in the country, according to *USA Today*. The team's only loss came in the final game of the Chicago city championship. Nick, who had grown to 6-6, averaged 20.5 points, 10.5 rebounds, five assists and four blocked shots. He was named "Mr. Basketball" in Illinois and accepted a full athletic scholarship to the University of Illinois—the same school Benjy had hoped to attend.

At first the transition was difficult for Nick. He struggled academically and had to sit out his freshman year. Eventually, though, he adapted to the challenges of the classroom and became a good student. He also became one of the best players in college basketball. And he never forgot his roots. In honor of Benjy, Nick chose to wear No. 25 for the Fighting Illini.

"Benjy wore 25 in high school," Nick says. "I don't forget the people who have inspired me and who have been good friends to me."

Along with teammate Kendall Gill, who would also become an NBA star, Nick led Illinois to the NCAA Final Four in 1989. The Fighting Illini lost to eventual champion Michigan by two points in the semifinals. A few months later Nick was selected by the Orlando Magic in the first round of the NBA Draft. Orlando was an expansion team at the time, and Nick was the first player drafted in the history of the franchise. It was a good choice. Nick averaged 11.5 points as a rookie. Two years later he was the team's leading scorer with an average of 19.9 points. Over the next two seasons the Magic added two of the game's best players, Shaquille O'Neal and Penny Hardaway. Because he no longer had to carry most of the offensive burden, Nick became a more complete player. His rebounding and defensive skills improved, and the Magic became a better team. They made the play-offs for the first time in 1994, and reached the NBA Finals in 1995.

In the NBA, as in college, Nick wears jersey No. 25. Many years have passed since the death of

Benjamin Wilson, but a part of him lives on in Nick Anderson. "Every time I step on that basketball court, I am Benjy Wilson and Nick Anderson all in one," Nick says. "I've dedicated my whole career to him. I strive to be the best because I know he would have been the best in this league."

Nick has also turned out to be one of the NBA's better players. A smooth shooter who can play for-

Nick frequently visits schools to speak with children and inspire them to strive to do their best.

ward as well as guard, he is the Magic's career-scoring leader. But basketball is only part of his life. It is only one of his talents. In 1992 Nick helped create the Boyz from the Hood Foundation, which provides funding for urban athletic programs. He frequently visits schools to speak with children. His message is this: Life in the inner city can be tough, but it doesn't have to be a dead-end. Education is the key.

"I know this turf and I know it's hard," Anderson once told a group of Chicago school children. "But you have to be strong. Stay out of trouble and stay in school. I was just where you were. You can make it, too."

Nick Anderson

Height: 6-6 • Weight: 220 • Born: 1/20/68 • College: Illinois

Season	Team	G	FG%	FT%	STL	BLK	RPG	APG	PPG
89–90	Orlando	81	.494	.705	69	34	3.9	1.5	11.5
90–91	Orlando	70	.467	.668	74	44	5.5	1.5	14.1
91–92	Orlando	60	.463	.667	97	33	6.4	2.7	19.9
92–93	Orlando	79	.449	.741	128	56	6.0	3.4	19.9
93–94	Orlando	81	.478	.672	134	33	5.9	3.6	15.8
94–95	Orlando	76	.476	.704	125	22	4.4	4.1	15.8
95–96	Orlando	77	.442	.692	121	46	5.4	3.6	14.7
96–97	Orlando	63	.397	.404	120	32	4.8	2.9	12.0
Totals		**587**	**.459**	**.682**	**868**	**300**	**5.3**	**2.9**	**15.4**

"Because of what I've been through, I value life every day."

—Chris Gatling

CHRIS GATLING
NEVER QUIT

Chris Gatling's nickname is "The Energizer." In fact, he even wears a tattoo of the Energizer Bunny on his right arm. It's an appropriate symbol. Like the tireless rabbit, Chris just keeps on going . . . and going . . . and going. He doesn't know the meaning of the word quit.

That spirit and determination have helped make Chris, a 6-10 forward for the New Jersey Nets, one of the top frontcourt players in the NBA. He has excellent leaping ability and a soft touch with the basketball. Still, Chris would be the first person to admit that talent isn't everything. Sometimes you need a little luck—and courage.

"I tell people that you can't ever give up," he says. "You have to keep your willpower."

Chris knows all about adversity. In the spring of 1985 he was on top of the world. He had just finished his junior season at Elizabeth High School in Elizabeth, New Jersey, and it was already clear that he was one of the best basketball players in the state. His future was filled with promise: a college scholarship, maybe even a professional career. Anything seemed possible. But on April 13, all of Chris Gatling's plans were put on hold.

As he often did when he wasn't playing basketball or doing his schoolwork, Chris was helping out one rainy night at his father's construction company. One of his tasks was to wipe off the windshield of a large maintenance van. Chris climbed up on the bumper, just as he had on countless other occasions, and went to work. Suddenly, he lost his footing and slipped to the ground. He landed headfirst.

"I was unconscious for a moment, but came to," Chris says. "So I went back to the site and continued working. But I started to get really tired. And then I felt sick."

Chris doesn't recall much of what happened next. The past comes back to him in a haze. He remembers his father, Raymond, pleading with him to stay awake as they sped to the hospital. He remembers fighting with the doctors and nurses as they tried to strip off his clothes and shave his head. And he remembers someone telling him to count backward from 100.

By then the bad news had already been delivered to Raymond and his wife, Rebecca. Their son had suffered a severe injury. He needed emergency surgery to relieve the pressure and swelling on his brain. Without the operation, Chris would almost certainly die. There was nothing to do but hope and pray.

Chris lay in a coma for the next two and a half weeks. His parents stayed by his side the entire time. When he finally woke, he was paralyzed on the right side of his body. His speech was badly slurred. He also came down with pneumonia. Eventually, he was moved to a different hospital and had to endure a second operation. The paralysis faded. After three months he finally went home. Doctors told Chris he was lucky to be alive. They didn't even talk about basketball. There was no point. He'd probably never play again.

But Chris had other ideas.

"When I came out of the hospital I was right back out there on the court, shooting and messing around," he says. "My mother used to scream her head off at me."

No Sense Crying

Chris's recovery was remarkably swift. Within three months he was playing in a summer league. The following fall he was back in the starting line-up for Elizabeth High. After the 1985–86 season he was named New Jersey High School Player of the Year. Along the way Chris added dozens of hats to his wardrobe. They were given to him by friends who knew that Chris felt self-conscious about the scars on his head. After a while, though, he stopped wearing the hats.

"The scars are there for life," he says. "There's no sense crying about it."

Chris is a strong person. He doesn't believe
in feeling sorry for himself.

Chris was heavily recruited in his senior year.
He decided to attend the University of Pittsburgh,
but later changed his mind and transferred to Old
Dominion University in Virginia. He averaged 21.3
points at ODU, even though his career was inter-
rupted when he began experiencing dizzy spells.
Doctors performed another operation in which
they removed bone fragments and implanted a

steel-mesh plate in Chris's head. But through it all, Chris maintained a positive attitude.

Despite all he had been through, Chris made it to the NBA in 1991. He was a first-round draft pick of the Golden State Warriors and the sixteenth selected overall. It didn't take long for Chris to become one of the team's most popular players. In fact, after the 1993–94 season he was named the winner of the Jack McMahon Award, which is given each year to the Warriors' most inspirational player.

Chris played in every game that season and averaged 8.2 points. His best season with Golden State came in 1994–95, when he averaged 13.7 points and 7.6 rebounds. He also led the NBA in field goal percentage. The next year, while first playing for Golden State and then for the Miami Heat, Chris averaged 11.1 points and 5.9 rebounds.

The 1996–97 season was one of the best of Chris's career. It was also one of the worst. He left Miami in July and signed as a free agent with the Dallas Mavericks. But in February he was traded to the New Jersey Nets. Although Chris was happy and successful in Dallas, he welcomed the trade. After all, he had grown up in New Jersey. For both Chris and his family, it was the best possible news: He would be coming home! Now his parents would get to see him play more often. The timing was perfect, because Chris was playing extremely well. In fact, he had never played better. He averaged 19 points and 7.9 rebounds in 1996–97. He was even invited to play in the NBA All-Star Game for the first time.

Just as Chris was about to join the ranks of the NBA's best players, a new obstacle stood in his path.

Unfortunately, not long after he arrived in New Jersey, Chris began suffering from dizzy spells again. Even worse, he was experiencing numbness in his face. His eyes watered. His nose ran constantly. He couldn't talk properly. He couldn't smile. He couldn't even drink a glass of water without it dribbling down his chin. And, of course, he couldn't play basketball. It was almost as if someone had injected novocaine into his cheeks.

Doctors traced the problem to a severe inner ear infection, which caused nerve damage in Chris's face. They said the condition would almost certainly correct itself. But the recovery would take time. It was a frustrating period for Chris. He had been through so much and fought back on so many occasions. Now basketball was being taken away from him again, just as he was about to join the ranks of the NBA's best players. It didn't seem fair.

Chris missed the last two months of the 1996–97 season while recovering from his illness. He couldn't even work out with his new teammates. All he could do was watch . . . and wait. Fortunately, Chris is a strong person. He doesn't believe in feeling sorry for himself. So he expressed no bitterness over his situation. Instead, he kept a positive attitude.

"I've overcome obstacles in my life before," he said late in the season. "This is just another one."

Chris Gatling

Height: 6-10 • Weight: 230 • Born: 9/3/67 • College: Old Dominion

Season	Team	G	FG%	FT%	STL	BLK	RPG	APG	PPG
91-92	Golden State	54	.568	.661	31	36	3.4	0.3	5.7
92-93	Golden State	70	.539	.725	44	53	4.6	0.6	9.3
93-94	Golden State	82	.588	.620	40	63	4.8	0.5	8.2
94-95	Golden State	58	.633	.592	39	52	7.6	0.9	13.7
95-96	GS/Miami	71	.575	.672	36	40	5.9	0.6	11.1
96-97	Dal/NJ	47	.525	.717	39	31	7.9	0.6	19.0
Totals		**382**	**.570**	**.667**	**229**	**275**	**5.6**	**0.6**	**10.7**

"I have a different perspective on life now. I know how precious everyone's health is, how precious each day is."

—Steve Kerr

STEVE KERR

THE LONG
SHOT

January 18, 1984: The phone is ringing in Steve Kerr's dormitory room at the University of Arizona. It's nearly three in the morning. Steve, a freshman guard on the Wildcats' basketball team, picks up the receiver and mumbles a sleepy hello. On the other end of the line is a man named Vake Simonian, a close friend of the Kerr family. His voice is quiet, his tone serious.

"Steve," he says. "Your father has been shot."

Steve snaps to attention. Now fully awake, he gathers his thoughts. His father, Malcolm Kerr, is president of the American University in Beirut, Lebanon. Malcolm has spent much of his life in the war-torn Middle East, and his family has grown accustomed to the threats of violence and terrorism. Now, though, the reality of the situation is hitting close to home. Steve takes a deep breath.

"Is he all right?"

There is a long, dreadful pause. The silence tells Steve everything he needs to know. Everything he does not want to hear.

Finally, there is a response. "Your father was a great man."

Steve drops the phone and begins to cry.

Today Steve Kerr is a 6-3, 180-pound guard for the world-champion Chicago Bulls. He is a fierce competitor and one of the best long-range shooters in the NBA. With a wife and two small children, and a job with one of the most successful basketball franchises in history, he has a good life. But there are times when he wishes he could share his success with his father.

"He would have loved this," Steve says. "He would have tried to attend all my games."

Steve was born in Beirut on September 27, 1965. He was the third of four children born to Malcolm and Ann Kerr, who had met as students at the American University. Malcolm took a teaching position at UCLA when Steve was a child, and the whole family moved to Los Angeles.

Malcolm was a gentle, spirited man with a good sense of humor and a fondness for sports. He played pickup basketball with his kids and tutored them on the finer points of throwing and hitting a baseball. Steve turned out to be the most talented athlete in the family. But he was also the most temperamental. He would throw his bat after striking out, or storm off the court in tears after losing a game of one-on-one. Malcolm encouraged his son's passion, but always tried to make him realize that there was more to life than sports. Schoolwork was emphasized above all else in the

Kerr household. And no one, especially Steve, was allowed to have a big ego.

As Steve notes, "One of my father's favorite sayings was, 'You're a modest fellow, Steve. And you have a lot to be modest about.' He was kidding, but it wasn't entirely a joke. He wanted me to understand my place in the world."

A Humbling Experience

There were times when it was hard for Steve to know exactly what his place was, especially when it came to basketball. Although he was a good player at Pacific Palisades High School, he was recruited by just one Division I college team: Gonzaga University in Spokane, Washington. In the spring of his senior year, Steve visited Gonzaga and played pickup ball with some of the varsity players. It was not a memorable performance. For more than two hours he was humiliated by a skinny, little kid who looked like he didn't even belong on the court. It wasn't until later that Steve learned the kid's name: John Stockton, who would go on to become one of the greatest point guards in NBA history.

Gonzaga lost interest in Steve. But a few months later, while playing in a summer recreational league, he was spotted by a coach from the University of Arizona. The Wildcats were looking

Now after the tragic death of his father, Steve appreciates the time with his family and friends more than ever.

for a practice player, someone to fill out the roster, and they thought Steve could do the job. So they offered him a scholarship.

No one expected Steve to be anything more than a benchwarmer at Arizona. He was too frail and too slow. But he made up for his lack of physical ability by working harder than everyone else and by practicing for hours on his jump shot. Arizona Coach Lute Olson was impressed. Steve's playing time began to increase. By the middle of his freshman year, he was the first guard off the bench and he was averaging more than seven points a game. Everything seemed to be going well.

Then tragedy struck. His father was killed by an assassin while walking to class one day. Suddenly, the world seemed a much darker place to Steve. "I was an eighteen-year-old freshman in college," he says. "Nothing bad had ever happened to me. It was shocking. I had to grow up in a hurry."

With the help of his family and teammates, he did exactly that. But it wasn't easy. Just two days after his father's death, Steve stood on the sidelines and wept as the crowd observed a moment of silence for Malcolm Kerr. When Steve entered the game in the first half he immediately hit a 20-foot jump shot. He finished the game with 12 points, a career high at the time.

The loss of his father was terribly sad for Steve, but it also made him a stronger person. When the Wildcats played at arch-rival Arizona State, a group of mean-spirited students chanted, "Hey, Kerr, where's your dad?" during pregame warm-ups. Steve's blood boiled as he listened to them. But he used their taunts to motivate himself. Then he went out and scored 20 points in the first half.

Steve improved in each of his first three years at Arizona. He averaged 7.1 points as a freshman, 10 points as a sophomore and 14.4 points as a junior. In 1986, though, Steve seriously injured his knee and was forced to sit out an entire season. The type of injury Steve had sometimes ends a player's career. But he worked hard to rehabilitate the knee and get back in shape. In the fall of 1987 he returned to the Arizona lineup and helped lead the Wildcats to the NCAA Final Four.

After graduating from Arizona, Steve hoped to pursue a career in professional basketball. But some people thought he was too small and too slow to play in the NBA. He was taken by the Phoenix Suns late in the second round of the 1988 NBA Draft. For the next five years Steve bounced around the league. He played for the Cleveland Cavaliers and the Orlando Magic, as well as the Suns. He averaged only 4.5 points and often spent the entire game on the bench.

Steve's perseverance paid off when he signed with the Chicago Bulls.

It wasn't until 1993 that Steve's career began to blossom. After his contract with the Magic expired, he asked his agent to try to arrange a deal with the Bulls. Steve liked Chicago's famous triangle offense, which emphasized team play. He thought he would fit in well. As it turned out, he was absolutely right. Steve played in all 82 games and averaged a career-high 8.6 points in his first season in Chicago. Two years later he helped the Bulls win an NBA title.

Steve knows his role in Chicago. On a team that features superstars Michael Jordan and Scottie Pippen, he is not expected to be a scorer. His job is to play hard and pass the ball. But when teams try to double-team Jordan or Pippen, Steve is often left wide open. When that happens, Chicago's opponent is in trouble, because Steve is the NBA's career leader in three-point field goal percentage. He won the Long Distance Shootout during the 1997 NBA All-Star Weekend. He also clinched the 1997 NBA title for the Bulls by hitting the winning shot in Game 6 of the NBA Finals against the Utah Jazz.

"Steve knows where he has to be on the court," says Bulls Coach Phil Jackson. "And the other team knows that he can drain the outside shot. He makes everybody on defense have to stay home. That gives our other guys more room to operate."

It makes the Bulls a better team, which is all that matters to Steve Kerr. Despite his success and fame, he remains exceptionally modest and good-natured. His father would have been proud.

Steve Kerr

Height: 6-3 • Weight: 180 • Born: 9/27/65 • College: Arizona

Season	Team	G	FG%	FT%	STL	BLK	RPG	APG	PPG
88–89	Phoenix	26	.435	.667	7	0	0.7	0.9	2.1
89–90	Cleveland	78	.444	.863	45	7	1.3	3.2	6.7
90–91	Cleveland	57	.444	.849	29	4	0.6	2.3	4.8
91–92	Cleveland	48	.511	.833	27	10	1.6	2.3	6.6
92–93	Cleve.-Orl.	52	.434	.917	10	1	0.9	1.3	2.6
93–94	Chicago	82	.497	.856	75	3	1.6	2.6	8.6
94–95	Chicago	82	.527	.778	44	3	1.5	1.8	8.2
95–96	Chicago	82	.506	.929	63	2	1.3	2.3	8.4
96–97	Chicago	82	.533	.806	67	3	1.6	2.1	8.1
Totals		**589**	**.495**	**.847**	**367**	**33**	**1.3**	**2.2**	**6.8**

"I understand what it's like for a kid to be trapped behind four walls."

—Reggie Miller

REGGIE MILLER

WILLPOWER

37

With his willowy frame and boyish face, Reggie Miller might look like a pushover. But he's not. The 6-7, 185-pound guard for the Indiana Pacers is one of the most confident and colorful players in the NBA. He likes to chat with his opponents while he's on the basketball court because he feels it gives him a mental advantage. And he likes to shoot from outside —way outside!—because that's where he feels most comfortable.

"Sometimes, when things are going right," Reggie says, "I feel like I can will the ball into the basket."

In his 10-year professional career, Reggie has earned a reputation as one of the game's best long-range shooters. He is the first player in NBA history to make more than 100 three-point field goals in seven consecutive seasons. In 1996–97, he led the league in three-pointers. Some nights it seems as though there is no shot too long for Reggie. He simply pulls up from 25 or 30 feet and lets the ball fly.

Reggie's success can be traced back to his childhood in Riverside, California, to a time when he wondered whether he'd ever get a chance to play basketball. Born on August 24, 1965, he was the fourth of five children raised by Saul and

Carrie Miller. Saul was a sergeant in the U.S. Air Force; Carrie was a nurse. They were devoted parents who believed in providing their children with direction and discipline as well as love.

The Millers were always busy with schoolwork, household chores and sports. In fact, several of the children became exceptional athletes. Cheryl played basketball for the University of Southern California, led the United States to a gold medal at the 1984 Olympics, and is a member of the Basketball Hall of Fame. Darrell played professional baseball with the California Angels for five years. Reggie's younger sister, Tammy, was a volleyball player at Cal-State Fullerton. And Saul, Jr., the oldest child, "was probably the best athlete of all of us," notes Reggie. "But he chose to go into the Air Force."

Reggie, of course, has become the most famous of the Miller children. When he was a little boy, though, he was nothing more than a spectator in the family's spirited backyard basketball games. When Reggie was born, his hips were badly twisted and deformed, causing his legs and ankles to turn inward. The defect was so severe that doctors told Saul and Carrie their son would probably never walk without a limp. They said there was no chance that he'd be able to play sports.

For the first five years of his life Reggie wore

steel leg braces and corrective shoes. While his siblings played basketball, he sat at the window and watched. It was a hard time for the entire family. But the Millers remained confident and upbeat. They kept telling Reggie that the doctors were wrong.

"My mother would always say, 'You'll be out there soon, honey. You've just got to get your legs stronger,'" Reggie remembers. "She was so optimistic. My parents never told me anything negative. They said, 'You will walk. You will run. You will play basketball.' They weren't going to let it affect the rest of my life."

Sibling Rivalry

With persistence and the support of his family, Reggie shed his braces just as he was about to enter grade school. Before long he was playing hoops in the backyard with his brothers and sisters. It was there that he began to develop the attitude that now serves him so well in the NBA.

Competition was fierce in the Miller home. And it was honest. No one ever went easy on Reggie just because he was smaller and younger. If he tried to take the ball inside against Cheryl, who was a year and a half older and several inches taller, she swatted it back in his face. In time Reggie realized that if he wanted to compete with his siblings, he'd have to move away from the basket. So he began to work on his jump shot.

He practiced for hours on end, until his arms ached and his hands blistered. Eventually Reggie's range exceeded the boundaries of the concrete slab that served as the family basketball court. But he kept moving back, until he found himself launching bombs from his mother's rose garden, 25 feet from the basket. Carrie Miller tried to put a stop to that. She ordered Reggie to stay on the court. But sometimes he would creep back. He couldn't help it. He loved shooting—the farther the better. He loved the feel of the ball as it left his hands and the sound it made as it slipped through the net.

Reggie practiced until his hands blistered. Then he practiced some more.

"Learning to shoot over people—that's just part of playing with older people," Reggie says. "You have to develop a quick release and a high-arching shot. I had to come up with every advantage I could."

Reggie was only 5-9 when he was a freshman in high school, but he became one of the best players in California. His appearance was deceptive.

Although bone thin, Reggie was extraordinarily tough. If he was knocked down by a bigger player or if one of his shots was blocked, he just worked harder. He never quit. He never backed down from a confrontation. And when his jump shot was falling, he was practically unstoppable.

No matter how much Reggie accomplished, though, he was always overshadowed by Cheryl. By the time she was a senior, Cheryl was considered the best female high school player in the country. Everyone knew her name. Reggie was just "Cheryl's kid brother." One night Reggie came home from a road game and proudly declared that he had scored 39 points. It was the best game of his career. He wanted nothing more than to brag about it in front of his big sister. But Cheryl had also played that evening. In fact, she had scored 105 points!

"Reggie had to handle a lot of difficult things at an early age," says Cheryl. "And I was probably one of them. But I think it helped him. The big thing he's learned is that there's no obstacle too big to overcome."

Of course, having Cheryl in the family wasn't all bad. Sometimes Reggie would take his sister to a local playground and hustle games of two-on-two. They didn't look like much of a team—a skinny kid and a girl—but they rarely lost. After a while,

Reggie's parents told him, over and over: "You will walk. You will run. You will play basketball."

when people began to recognize Cheryl, they had to take their show on the road.

Like Cheryl, Reggie decided to attend college in his hometown. He accepted a scholarship from the University of California at Los Angeles, where he averaged 17.4 points. Opposing fans often taunted Reggie with cries of "Cheryl! Cheryl!" but he ignored them. Reggie's concentration was so strong that he was able to make 54.7 percent of his field goal attempts in college—an impressive figure for a guard.

Reggie was chosen by the Pacers in the first round of the 1987 NBA Draft. Since then he has proved to be one of professional basketball's toughest competitors. He's played in three NBA All-Star Games and helped lead the United States Dream Team to a gold medal at the 1996 Summer Olympics in Atlanta.

Reggie has averaged 19.8 points in his NBA career. He's a consistent player, but he's at his best in pressure situations. For example, his scoring average in playoff games is 24.7. In Game 5 of the 1994 Eastern Conference Finals, he scored 25 points in the fourth quarter to lead the Pacers to a dramatic victory over the New York Knicks. It was an amazing performance. The crowd at New York's Madison Square Garden booed Reggie mercilessly. The Knicks did everything in their power to stop him. They double-teamed him; they triple-teamed him. But Reggie kept firing . . . and hitting!

"This game is ninety percent mental and ten percent physical," Reggie says. "There's lots of pressure. I've never been the biggest or strongest player, but I've been able to make things work for me."

Reggie Miller

Height: 6-7 • Weight: 185 • Born: 8/24/65 • College: UCLA

Season	Team	G	FG%	FT%	STL	BLK	RPG	APG	PPG
87–88	Indiana	82	.488	.801	53	19	2.3	1.6	10.0
88–89	Indiana	74	.479	.844	93	29	3.9	3.1	16.0
89–90	Indiana	82	.514	.868	110	18	3.6	3.8	24.6
90–91	Indiana	82	.512	.918	109	13	3.4	4.0	22.6
91–92	Indiana	82	.501	.858	105	26	3.9	3.8	20.7
92–93	Indiana	82	.479	.880	120	26	3.1	3.2	21.2
93–94	Indiana	79	.503	.908	119	24	2.7	3.1	19.9
94–95	Indiana	81	.462	.897	98	16	2.6	3.0	19.6
95–96	Indiana	76	.473	.863	77	13	2.8	3.3	21.1
96–97	Indiana	80	.443	.878	75	25	3.5	3.4	21.6
Totals		**800**	**.485**	**.877**	**959**	**209**	**3.2**	**3.2**	**19.7**

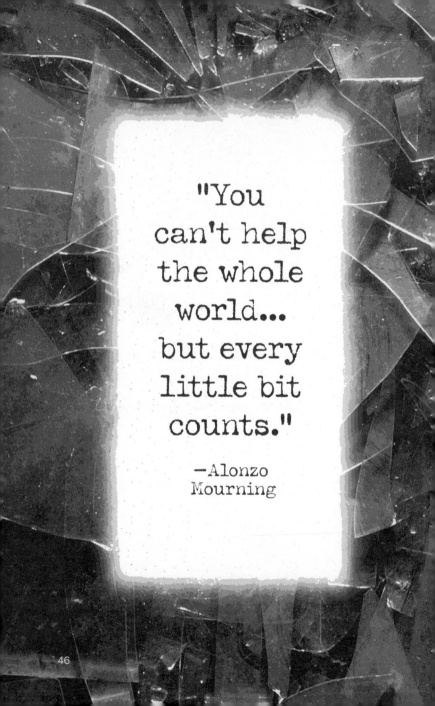

"You can't help the whole world... but every little bit counts."

—Alonzo Mourning

46

ALONZO MOURNING

FOSTER CHILD

There are two sides to Miami Heat center Alonzo Mourning. There is the public side—the man known as "Zo," with bulging biceps and a thickly muscled chest. He is a ferocious, scowling competitor who intimidates opponents with his physical strength and fearless attitude.

And then there is the other Alonzo—the one who can brighten an entire room with his smile. The one who is quick to kneel and help a child as he or she fumbles with shoelaces—the gentle giant.

"Basketball is a business," Alonzo says. "I go out there wearing my game face every time. But I'm not always like that."

At 6-10, 260 pounds, Alonzo is one of the strongest players in the NBA. But he knows how it feels to be weak, to be frightened. There are memories from his childhood that he'll never shake, no matter how old he gets or how much he accomplishes. They will always be with him.

"I come from a broken home," Alonzo says. "Some of the things I went through in that period weren't easy at all. It's unfortunate that I had to start in that type of situation, but I learned from it."

Alonzo was born on February 8, 1970, in Chesapeake, Virginia. His childhood was difficult, mainly because his parents were always fighting. The situation in his home was so bad that Alonzo was placed in the state's foster care system. For several years he bounced from one home to another. Because he never knew how long he would be in one place, he found it difficult to make friends. He was quiet and shy. And he was lonely.

Until he met Fannie Threet.

In addition to her own family, Fannie has adopted 11 children and provided food and shelter for more than 200 others over the past 50 years. She is a remarkable woman who has devoted her life to helping needy children. When 10-year-old Alonzo found himself in Fannie's care, he instantly fell in love. For the first time, he felt like he had a home and he didn't want to leave.

"Alonzo just took to Mom," Fannie's son, Robert, once told the *Sacramento Bee*. "She has a way of making people feel comfortable. And she doesn't know how to say no."

It wasn't long before Alonzo also began calling Fannie "Mom." He thrived under her care. He became more confident and secure. When he needed a place to vent his anger and aggression, he turned to the basketball court. In Fannie Threet's home Alonzo was a sweet, even-tempered boy. With a basketball in his hands, though, he was a fierce competitor.

By the time he was a senior at Chesapeake's Indian River High School, Alonzo was one of the most heavily recruited players in the nation. He could have attended almost any college, but he decided to accept a scholarship to Georgetown University in nearby Washington, D.C. That way he would be close enough to visit Fannie when-

---

Alonzo found a second home at Georgetown, under the leadership of Coach John Thompson.

---

ever he wanted. Alonzo also wanted to play for Georgetown Coach John Thompson, who had a reputation for bringing out the best in young men who had grown up under difficult circumstances.

Georgetown was the right choice for Alonzo. In 1989, as a freshman, he averaged 13.1 points and 7.3 rebounds. He also led the NCAA in blocked shots with an average of 4.97 per game. As a sophomore he averaged 16.5 points and 8.5 rebounds and was named Second-Team All-America.

Alonzo could have jumped to the NBA after his sophomore or junior season, but elected instead to stay in school. It was a wise decision. Not only did he graduate from Georgetown with a degree in sociology, he improved as a basketball player. Alonzo was one of the top centers in college basketball as a senior. He averaged 21.3 points and 10.7 rebounds. An intimidating presence in the middle, he again led the NCAA in blocked shots; in fact, Alonzo finished his career as the NCAA's career leader in blocked shots with 453. He became the first player in Big East Conference history to win conference awards for Player of the Year, Defensive Player of the Year and Tournament Most Valuable Player.

Making an Impact

The Charlotte Hornets selected Alonzo with the second pick in the 1992 NBA Draft. Although he had been successful in college, some people wondered whether Alonzo was big enough to play center in the NBA. After all, he'd often be competing against players who were several inches taller. It wasn't long, however, before Alonzo proved that he could handle himself. He averaged 21 points and 10.3 rebounds in his first season, and was named to the NBA All-Rookie first team. But it was on defense that his impact was most obvious. Alonzo blocked 271 shots as a rookie—more than the entire Charlotte team had accumulated in the previous two seasons combined!

Alonzo averaged 21.5 points in the 1993–94 season, but he also missed 22 games because of injuries. The lost time made Alonzo realize that he needed to become stronger to endure the rigors of a long NBA season. So he adopted a new approach to health and fitness. He eliminated red meat from his diet. He stopped eating fried foods and cut back on sugar. And he began spending at least two hours a day in the weight room. The results were obvious. Alonzo's body became lean and sculpted. His stamina and strength increased. Before long he was one of the fittest players in the NBA.

In the summer of 1994 Alonzo helped the United States win a gold medal at the World Championship of Basketball. The next season he led the Hornets to a 50–32 record—the best mark in the franchise's history. Alonzo was first on the team in scoring (21.3) and rebounding (9.9).

Alonzo never forgets his roots, never forgets how it feels to be alone, or frightened.

But it wasn't just his performance on the basketball court that made Alonzo one of the most popular athletes in Charlotte. It was what he did away from the court. In 1994 Alonzo took part in an NBA tour of South Africa. Along with fellow Georgetown alumni Patrick Ewing and Dikembe Mutombo, he visited schools and gave clinics that thrilled children all across the country.

At home he was equally active. Alonzo embraced causes that were close to his heart. For example, he became the NBA's national spokesman for the prevention of child abuse. During one particularly emotional television commercial, he read a letter from a woman who had been abused as a child and who feared that she would treat her own children the same way.

"Society needs to wake up and understand that we have problems," Alonzo says. "There are many good causes out there, but you can't help everybody. I decided to select one cause and be really true to it. Because I'm a celebrity I can bring attention to this cause. And because I can relate to what these kids are going through, I can talk to them and tell them that it's going to be all right."

Alonzo was not just a spokesman. He was a frequent visitor at the Thompson's Children's Home in Charlotte. He would stop in and read to the children, play with them, act like a big brother.

He often provided T-shirts, sneakers and other clothing.

"I can relate to their situation," Alonzo says. "I didn't experience some of the things these kids have been through, but I know how it feels to grow up in a foster home. I know that it's painful when you're not in the same house as your mother and father. I just want them to understand that there are people in the world who care about them."

Fans in Charlotte were disappointed when Alonzo left the Hornets in 1995 and signed a contract with the Miami Heat. But he has proved to be just as dedicated and popular in his new home. Alonzo has averaged more than 20 points and 10 rebounds since joining the Heat. In 1997 he led Miami to the Eastern Conference Finals of the NBA Playoffs. And he continues to devote time and energy to his favorite cause. Alonzo founded Zo's Summer Groove, a charity banquet, concert and celebrity basketball game. And each time he blocks a shot, he donates $100 to the Children's Home Society and Jackson Memorial Hospital.

During the 1996–97 season Alonzo swatted away 189 shots. He may not have smiled much, but he made a lot of people happy.

**NICK
ANDERSON**

CHRIS
GATLING

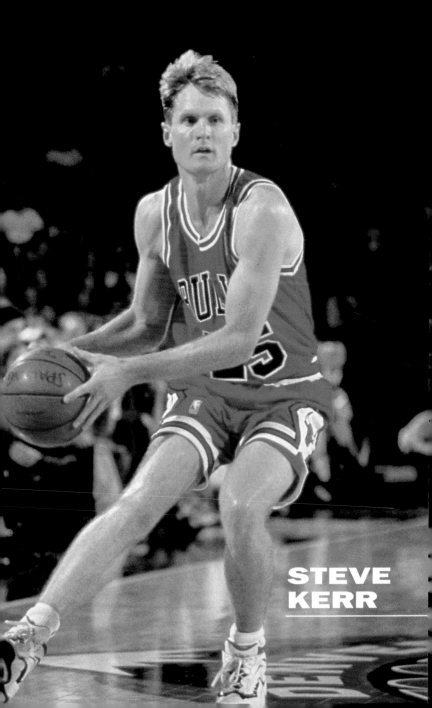

STEVE
KERR

REGGIE
MILLER

ALONZO
MOURNING

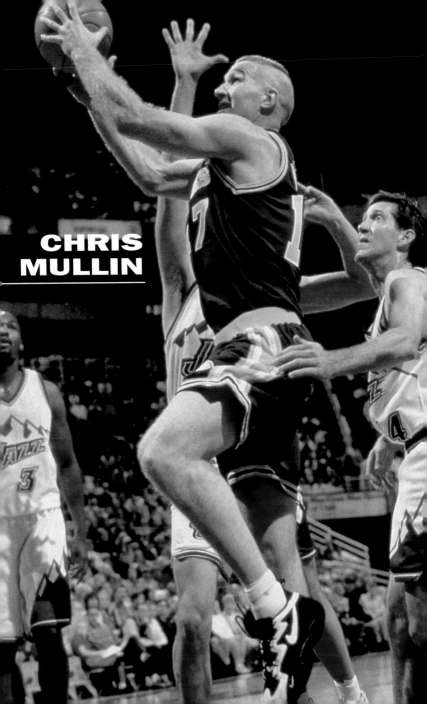

CHRIS
MULLIN

CARLOS ROGERS

JAYSON
WILLIAMS

Alonzo Mourning

Height: 6-10 • Weight: 260 • Born: 2/8/70 • College: Georgetown

Season	Team	G	FG%	FT%	STL	BLK	RPG	APG	PPG
92–93	Charlotte	78	.511	.781	27	271	10.3	1.0	21.0
93–94	Charlotte	60	.505	.762	27	188	10.2	1.4	21.5
94–95	Charlotte	77	.519	.761	49	225	9.9	1.4	21.3
95–96	Miami	70	.523	.685	70	189	10.4	2.3	23.2
96–97	Miami	66	.534	.642	56	189	9.9	1.6	19.8
Totals		**351**	**.519**	**.727**	**229**	**1062**	**10.1**	**1.5**	**21.4**

"Being a recovering alcoholic is part of my life. I can never forget it."

—Chris Mullin

CHRIS MULLIN

ONE DAY AT A TIME

Chris Mullin knew he was in trouble. He was 30 pounds overweight and struggling to keep up with his teammates during a workout. He was one of the youngest players on the Golden State Warriors. He was also one of the team's biggest stars. But he hadn't been taking care of himself, and now he was paying the price. As his teammates continued to run, Chris stepped off the court and threw up.

It was a humiliating experience. But the worst was yet to come. On December 10, 1987, Chris was suspended by the Warriors after he missed a practice session. A few days later he was placed on the team's injured list. Chris wasn't really injured, though. He was sick. His disease was alcoholism, and he desperately needed help.

With his parents by his side, Chris flew to Los Angeles and entered a treatment program. In the lobby of the hospital he held his father's hand and choked back tears.

"Don't worry," Rod Mullin said to his son. "It will be all right."

Chris Mullin was born on July 30, 1963, in New York. A self-proclaimed "gym rat," Chris was happiest when he had a basketball in his hands. He spent hours perfecting his left-handed jump shot on the playgrounds of Brooklyn and Manhattan. He was always looking for a game.

Chris's love for the sport paid off. By the time he graduated from Xaverian High School, he was one of the top young players in the country. He was recruited by dozens of Division I college programs. But Chris was a New Yorker. He loved the city. And he loved his family. He couldn't imagine leaving his parents and four brothers and sisters behind. So he decided to attend St. John's University in New York City.

Chris adapted easily to the college game. In fact, he became one of the best players in St. John's history. He graduated as the school's all-time leading scorer with 2,440 points. In 1984, after his junior year, he helped lead the United States basketball team to a gold medal at the Summer Olympics in Los Angeles. In 1985 he was named Player of the Year in college basketball.

At the 1985 NBA Draft, the Golden State Warriors selected Chris with the seventh pick overall. It was a thrilling moment for Chris and his family. But it was also a sad moment. Chris had dreamed of playing professional basketball in New York. Instead, he would be playing 3,000 miles away, in Oakland, California. "It was hard for Chris," says his wife, Liz. "He had so many friends at St. John's. He had his family. All of a sudden he was all alone. He had to grow up—fast."

At first, Chris seemed to handle the transition well. In his first NBA game he hit a basket in the final minute to lead the Warriors over the Seattle SuperSonics! At 6-7, 215 pounds, he could play guard or forward. He had a soft shooting touch and great passing ability. He liked to score, but he was unselfish. In his first season Chris shot .896 from the free throw line, the second-highest percentage ever by an NBA rookie. The next year he played in every game and averaged 15.1 points. His career seemed to be going well.

Hurting Inside

In his heart, though, Chris was not happy. The Warriors were struggling on the court. Some of the players did not get along with one another. Chris felt out of place and lonely. He missed his friends and family. He was homesick. To ease the pain, Chris began to drink heavily.

At first, most people didn't realize that he had a problem. In the first two months of the 1987–88 season he averaged 17.6 points and 4.6 assists. But those closest to Chris recognized that something was wrong. He was bloated and out of shape, which is why he lagged behind in practice. He often stayed out all night and slept during the day. He was depressed.

It took a lot of hard work, but Chris has made the commitment to turn his life around.

One day coach Don Nelson confronted Chris. He suggested that Chris had a problem and challenged him to stop drinking for six months. Chris accepted the challenge, but within a few days he was drinking again. The Warriors finally suspended him, and soon Chris was on his way to a rehabilitation center. It helped that he had the support of his friends and family, especially his father, who was also a recovering alcoholic. Chris knew that sobriety made Rod Mullin a better person, and he hoped it would have a similar effect on him.

"When my dad stopped drinking, he became a lot more patient," Chris says. "Everything improved for him."

The same was true for Chris. After 28 days he was released from the alcohol treatment program at Centinela Hospital. He had a new look—a crew cut—and a new attitude. He realized that he had been wasting his talent. So he decided to get in the best shape of his life. On the day he left the hospital, Chris drove to a nearby gym and worked out for 90 minutes with the Warriors' conditioning coach. At the end of the session Chris decided to shoot some free throws. Although he hadn't touched a basketball in nearly a month, his touch was still golden. He made 91 straight shots before missing!

Exercise soon became a habit for Chris. He worked out constantly. He lifted weights. He ran. He rode a stationary bike. He even took up swimming. And, of course, he played basketball. Sometimes he worked out three or four times in a single day. He was always the first one to arrive at practice and the last one to leave. He became a role model for the rest of the Warriors.

"Two things happened when Chris made the

commitment to turn his life around," Don Nelson once said. "First, we wanted to keep him on the team. Second, he gave us a piece to build around."

By the end of the 1987–88 season Chris had shed all of his excess flab. He was back to his college weight of 215 pounds. And he was much leaner and more muscular. He was stronger. He soon

---

Chris left the treatment program with a new attitude. The gym rat was back and better than ever.

---

became one of the few players in the NBA who could play 48 minutes—an entire game—every night.

As his fitness improved, so did Chris's performance on the basketball court. In the final 44 games of the 1987–88 season he averaged 20.6 points. The following year he was one of the league's top players. He averaged a career-high 26.5 points, 5.1 assists and 5.9 rebounds, and was invited to play in the NBA All-Star Game for the first time. That was also the first of five consecutive seasons in which Chris averaged at least 25 points and five rebounds. In the 1990–91 and 1991–92 seasons he led the league in minutes played. He was named to the All-NBA First Team in 1992.

That summer he helped lead the United States Dream Team to a gold medal at the Summer Olympics in Barcelona, Spain.

The next few seasons were more difficult for Chris. He had a series of injuries that limited his playing time. In 1996–97, though, he was healthy. He played in 79 games and averaged 14.5 points. In his younger days Chris might have had trouble dealing with the difficulties he's encountered in recent years. But sobriety has given him perspective. Basketball, he says, is an important part of his life, but it is not the only thing that matters. After all, he is a husband and father now, with three small children.

"Basketball used to dictate everything," Chris says. "If I had a good game, I'd feel good about myself. If I had a bad game, I was down. Not anymore. Now if I have a bad game, I know it's just because I had an off night. I have a steady and consistent life now. I feel good."

Chris Mullin

Height: 6-7 • Weight: 215 • Born: 7/30/63 • College: St. John's

Season	Team	G	FG%	FT%	STL	BLK	RPG	APG	PPG
85-86	Golden State	55	.463	.896	70	23	2.1	1.9	14.0
86-87	Golden State	82	.514	.825	98	36	2.2	3.2	15.1
87-88	Golden State	60	.508	.885	113	32	3.4	4.8	20.2
88-89	Golden State	82	.509	.892	176	39	5.9	5.1	26.5
89-90	Golden State	78	.536	.889	123	45	5.9	4.1	25.1
90-91	Golden State	82	.536	.884	173	63	5.4	4.0	25.7
91-92	Golden State	81	.524	.833	173	62	5.6	3.5	25.6
92-93	Golden State	46	.510	.810	68	41	5.0	3.6	25.9
93-94	Golden State	62	.472	.753	107	53	5.6	5.1	16.8
94-95	Golden State	25	.489	.879	38	19	4.6	5.0	19.0
95-96	Golden State	55	.499	.856	75	32	2.9	3.5	13.3
96-97	Golden State	79	.553	.864	130	33	4.0	4.1	14.5
Totals		**787**	**.514**	**.862**	**1344**	**478**	**4.5**	**4.0**	**20.5**

"I'm a true believer that God would never give you anything you can't handle."

—Carlos Rogers

CARLOS ROGERS

BROTHERLY
LOVE

Carlos Rogers received the news in late January of 1997, shortly before the NBA All-Star break. His older sister, Rene, was ill. The kidney she had received in a transplant four years earlier was beginning to fail, and now she was suffering from a severe infection. Her life was in danger.

Carlos, a 6-11 forward for the Toronto Raptors, wasted no time. He walked into the office of then General Manager Isiah Thomas and said that he wanted to fly home to Detroit to be with his sister. But it wasn't just emotional support that Carlos wanted to offer. He had something much more precious in mind: He wanted to donate one of his own kidneys.

"I can't watch my sister suffer," Carlos said. "I have to do something for her."

Carlos realized that he was putting his own career at risk. With only one kidney, it was questionable whether he could continue to play professional basketball. But Carlos didn't care. He would do anything for Rene.

"If I have to save my sister's life, I'm not really concerned about my career," he told a group of reporters. "But Rene would never let me do it. So if I have to, I'll do it without her knowing. I believe my sister would rather die than for me to bring a halt to my basketball career."

The bond between Carlos and Rene ran deep. They grew up together in a Detroit ghetto, surrounded by crime and drugs and violence. Rene, three years older than Carlos, was a thoughtful and protective big sister. She tried to keep Carlos out of trouble. She encouraged him to stay in school. Rene saw in Carlos something that he rarely saw in himself: potential.

It wasn't easy for Carlos to have hope. There were 12 children in his family, and life in their cramped apartment was nearly as dangerous as life on the streets. Carlos's father was a drug addict who had a terrible temper. Sometimes he turned his rage on Carlos.

When Carlos was 10 years old, he had to jump out a second-story window to escape a beating. The abuse stopped only when his father left home.

Carlos's mother, Jacqueline, did the best she could to support her family. But there never seemed to be enough money or time. She worried constantly about her children—and with good reason. One of her sons, Kevin, was shot and killed when he was only 15. Carlos was robbed and beaten on several occasions.

Finally, at the age of 14, he decided that he would join a gang to protect himself. It worked, too. Other kids in the neighborhood left Carlos alone. But there was a price to pay. Carlos began selling drugs. He carried a gun. He became a criminal.

"I started doing stuff I had no business doing," Carlos remembers. "I was stealing from people and robbing from people. All I heard from my family was, 'You're going to end up dead.' But it got to the point where I didn't care."

Basketball Offers Hope

If not for basketball, Carlos might have ended up like his brother Kevin. He was introduced to the sport by his mother when he was nine years old. Jacqueline had been a high school basketball player and she enjoyed teaching the game to her children. Carlos had obvious talent. As a teenager he played pickup ball with some of the best high school players in Detroit, including future NBA stars Chris Webber and Jalen Rose.

But playground basketball was one thing. Organized basketball was something else entirely. Carlos often skipped school and hung out on the streets, so he didn't play varsity basketball until his senior year at Detroit Northwestern High School. Then everything began to change. Carlos grew six inches that year and caught the eye of college recruiters. He accepted a scholarship to the University of Arkansas at Little Rock.

Carlos was willing to do what it took to save his sister's life — even if it meant risking his career.

Because his grades were so low, Carlos was academically ineligible as a college freshman. The next year he played in 19 games and averaged 8.4 points. When one of his coaches left to take a job at Tennessee State University, Carlos decided to follow him. It was the best decision of his life. He averaged 20.3 points in 1992–93 and led the Tigers to the Ohio Valley Conference championship. The next season he averaged 24.5 points and 11.5 rebounds and was named conference player of the year. He was also named Second-Team All-America by *The Sporting News*. Carlos had his best college game in the final of the Ohio Valley Conference tournament. He scored 38 points and grabbed 14 rebounds as Tennessee State beat Murray State to qualify for the NCAA Tournament.

By then Carlos was considered one of the best players in college basketball. At the 1994 NBA Draft, the Seattle SuperSonics selected Carlos in the first round, with the 11th pick overall. But before the season began, he was traded to the Golden State Warriors.

Carlos's first year in the NBA was a disappointment. He played in only 49 games and averaged less than nine points. The following year he was traded to the Raptors, an expansion team about to play its first season in the NBA. Carlos began the year as a starter at small forward, but ended up playing a reserve role. He averaged 7.7 points and 3 rebounds in 56 games.

In his third season Carlos improved dramatically. Under new Head Coach Darrell Walker, he began to blossom as a player. He started shooting the ball better. He was more aggressive. His playing time increased. Suddenly Carlos looked like the great all-around athlete he had been at Tennessee State. Everything seemed to be going so well....

And then his sister got sick.

It wasn't the first time. Rene had endured kidney trouble since high school, and had undergone a transplant in 1992. Carlos was the only family member who was a compatible donor. At the time,

---

When Rene got sick, Carlos rushed to her side.

---

though, Rene refused to allow him to donate one of his kidneys. Rene had to take stronger medication designed to prevent her body from rejecting the new organ. Unfortunately, the medication weakened her immune system and left her susceptible to infection. So, when she became ill again, Carlos was quick to rush to her aid.

Rene's illness became public in late January of 1997, when Carlos wore a wristband bearing the words 4 RENE during a game against the Minnesota Timberwolves. Afterward, when reporters asked him what the message meant, he explained. His sister was sick, and he would do whatever was necessary to help her. Even if it meant risking his basketball career.

Sadly, Carlos never got the chance to help Rene.

She developed a serious blood infection and was much too weak to withstand another transplant. Carlos flew home to Detroit to be with his sister, but there was nothing he could do. On January 24, 1997, Rene Rogers died. The next day, at a memorial service, Carlos placed the wristband bearing Rene's name into her casket.

"My sister fought a long and hard battle," Carlos said. "Everything I do now is for her."

He wasn't referring simply to basketball. Carlos even promised to actively encourage others to become involved in organ donation programs. It was a cause that obviously meant a lot to Rene. She had been a student at Wayne State University and hoped to enter medical school. She wanted to be a kidney specialist. She wanted to use her own experience to help others. Now, in some way, Carlos can help Rene achieve that goal.

"I'm not going to let what my sister went through be in vain," he said.

Carlos Rogers

Height: 6-11 • Weight: 220 • Born: 2/6/71 • College: Tennessee State

Season	Team	G	FG%	FT%	STL	BLK	RPG	APG	PPG
94-95	Golden State	49	.529	.521	22	52	5.7	0.8	8.9
95-96	Toronto	56	.517	.546	25	48	3.0	0.6	7.7
96-97	Toronto	56	.525	.600	42	69	5.4	0.7	9.8
Totals		**161**	**.524**	**.558**	**89**	**169**	**4.7**	**0.7**	**8.8**

"I've already been through the worst. Things can only get better from here."

—Jayson Williams

JAYSON WILLIAMS

FATHER FIGURE

There was a time when Jayson Williams thought about quitting. It was the fall of his junior year at St. John's University, and the world was closing in on him. Two of his sisters had died of AIDS, and each had left behind a small child. Jayson, a devoted uncle, wanted to raise the children as if they were his own. But he was barely an adult himself. The pressure was overwhelming. Between basketball, schoolwork and family obligations, there never seemed to be enough hours in the day. Jayson was exhausted. Something had to give.

One day Jayson and his father walked into the office of St. John's Coach Lou Carnesecca. Jayson told the coach that he planned to leave school. There would be no more basketball, no more studying. Instead, he would go to work for his father's construction company. Carnesecca listened patiently. When Jayson finished, the coach told him he was making a mistake.

"Jayson," he said, "you have the talent to play in the NBA."

Jayson was barely listening. He had made up his mind. All of a sudden, though, his father began to weep.

"Dad said I made him proud when he saw me on TV and saw the Williams name up there on the screen," Jayson once told *Sports Illustrated*. "It was the only time in my whole life I ever saw my father cry. I knew then that I couldn't quit."

Today Jayson Williams is a 6-10, 245-pound center-forward in the NBA. His specialty is rebounding; in fact, he's one of the top rebounders in the league. That seems appropriate, since Jayson has been bouncing back his whole life.

He was born February 22, 1968, in Ritter, South Carolina, and grew up in New York City. Jayson was born into a large, diverse family. His mother, Barbara Williams, was a white Italian Catholic woman from New York who had two daughters from a previous marriage. His father, Elijah Joshua Williams, was a southern black man who had five children from a previous marriage.

The Williams family settled into a crowded apartment on the Lower East Side of Manhattan. It was a rough, dangerous neighborhood. Other children often made fun of Jayson because he had a speech impediment. The fact that he was biracial also led to problems. Some children taunted and insulted Jayson. They called him names and tried to provoke fights. Usually Jayson simply walked away. But the pain went with him.

Jayson spent a lot of time with his father when he was growing up. In the summer months he often accompanied his dad to work. He learned a lot about the construction business; he even learned how to drive a dump truck and a bulldozer. It was Jayson's mother, though, who first taught him how to play basketball. Before long he was one of the best young players in New York City. As a junior at Christ the King High School, Jayson sprouted to 6-7, 185 pounds. He attracted college scouts from all over the country. But when it came time to choose a school, Jayson decided to accept a scholarship from St. John's, in New York City. He wanted to stay close to home, to help his parents and his family, because they had been through some very hard times in recent years.

A Terrible Loss

In 1980 Jayson's older sister, Linda, who lived across the street, was attacked and beaten by a stranger as she entered her apartment. Linda lost so much blood that she nearly died. Transfusions saved her life. Unfortunately, the blood she received was tainted by the AIDS virus, and Linda soon became quite sick. To deal with the pain and loneliness of her illness, Linda began using drugs. She sometimes shared the experience with her younger sister, Laura. They also shared needles, and in that way Linda's disease was passed on to Laura.

Linda died of AIDS in 1983, at the age of 26. She left behind her four-year-old son, Ejay. Five years

Jayson believes all of his struggles have made him a stronger person today.

later Laura died. She left her 14-year-old daughter, Monique. For Jayson, it was almost too much to bear. He loved his sisters dearly, and now they were gone. To him, the world seemed a terribly unfair place.

"I was mad," Jayson says. "I couldn't understand why all these things were happening to my family."

Because he was often distracted and depressed,

Jayson was an inconsistent college player. He was academically ineligible as a freshman, and as a sophomore he averaged only 9.9 points. In his junior year, though, Jayson improved dramatically. Just a few months after Laura's death, he decided to stay in school and devote himself fully to the game of basketball. The hard work paid off. Jayson averaged 19.5 points and 7.9 rebounds, and was named Most Valuable Player of the National Invitation Tournament.

Unfortunately, Jayson suffered a broken foot in his senior year and played in only 14 games. As a result, he wasn't taken until late in the first round of the 1990 NBA Draft. Jayson was selected by the Phoenix Suns, but was traded to the Philadelphia 76ers before the start of the 1990–91 season. Shortly after signing his first professional contract, Jayson did something remarkable: He adopted both Ejay and Monique. It was an act of pure love, but it carried with it a tremendous amount of responsibility. Suddenly Jayson was not only an NBA rookie, but a father!

The strain was obvious during Jayson's first few years in the NBA. He played less than 10 minutes per game as a rookie and averaged only 3.5 points. In his second season he averaged 4.1 points. After the 1991–92 season Jayson was traded to the New Jersey Nets. The move brought him closer to home, so he didn't mind. But in his first year with the Nets, Jayson dislocated his ankle and played in only 12 games. He played in 70 games during the 1993–94 season and 75 the following year. But his performance was unsteady. He averaged less than five points. He developed a reputation as a poor foul shooter and defender. And he got in fights— both on and off the court.

Nothing seemed to be going right.

"I've been through a lot of things in my life," Jayson says. "I've had a lot to overcome. But it's made me a stronger person."

Jayson rescued his career by making a new commitment to the game. He changed his attitude. He stopped worrying about points and headlines and decided to concentrate on some of the less glamorous aspects of the game—like rebounding.

In Jayson's first few years in the NBA, nothing seemed to go right.

"I know that I have to go out there and play harder than the next man, because I'm not as talented," Jayson says. "That's the only way I can play. I've got to give it my all. That's why I like rebounding. You have to be mentally strong. You have to be willing to go out there and do the dirty work."

Jayson's new attitude has served him well. In

the 1995–96 season he averaged 9 points and 10 rebounds, even though he usually played only half the game. In 1996–97 he continued to improve. Midway through the season he was averaging 15.3 rebounds, second only to Chicago's Dennis Rodman. On February 6 he played one of the best games of his career. He had 21 points and 20 rebounds in a game against the Indiana Pacers. What made that performance really special was the fact that Jayson was playing with a badly injured hand. In fact, just one month later he underwent surgery to repair torn ligaments in his thumb. Jayson missed the rest of the season, but still had his best year. He averaged 13.4 points and 13.5 rebounds.

Although basketball is a priority in his life and keeps him quite busy, Jayson still finds time to help others. He's used his money and his background in construction to help renovate inner-city apartment buildings in New Jersey. He also stages charity softball games for the benefit of the Tomorrow's Children's Institute. One of Jayson's other favorite activities is talking. He enjoys being interviewed, and he even hosts a live interactive broadcast on the Internet.

The name of the show is perfect for a guy who loves to rebound: *Jayson's Boardroom*.

Jayson Williams

Height: 6-10 • Weight: 245 • Born: 2/22/68 • College: St. John's

Season	Team	G	FG%	FT%	STL	BLK	RPG	APG	PPG
90–91	Philadelphia	52	.447	.661	9	6	2.1	0.3	3.5
91–92	Philadelphia	50	.364	.636	20	20	2.9	0.2	4.1
92–93	New Jersey	12	.457	.389	4	4	3.4	0.0	4.1
93–94	New Jersey	70	.427	.605	17	36	3.8	0.4	4.6
94–95	New Jersey	75	.461	.533	26	33	5.7	0.5	4.8
95–96	New Jersey	80	.423	.592	35	57	10.0	0.6	9.0
96–97	New Jersey	41	.409	.590	24	36	13.5	1.2	13.4
Totals		**380**	**.423**	**.590**	**135**	**192**	**6.2**	**0.5**	**6.3**

PHOTO: SUSAN LAYDEN

Joe Layden has written more than a dozen books for children and adults, including titles such as *Rising Stars of the NBA*; *Dribble, Shoot, Score!*; *NBA Slam Dunk Champions*; and *NBA Game Day*, which he co-authored. He is also the author of *Women in Sports: The Complete Book on the World's Greatest Female Athletes* and *Notre Dame Football: A to Z*. Mr. Layden lives in Saratoga Springs, New York, with his wife, Susan, and their daughter, Emily.